Janet Pedersen

Millie
in the
Meadow

CANDLEWICK PRESS
CAMBRIDGE, MASSACHUSETTS

Millie was happy in the meadow.
She had plenty of grass to munch
and lots of flowers to smell.
Best of all, Millie was
surrounded by her many
colorful friends.

One day, an artist came to the meadow.

Millie watched as he squeezed out bright, cheerful colors.

Maybe he will paint a picture of me! Millie thought.

First, the artist painted someone
with a small red body
and black spots.

That's not me, Millie thought.

Millie swished her tail
and guessed.
Mooooo!
Must be Ladybug!

Next, the artist painted someone
with a round purple body and
1, 2, 3, 4, 5, 6, 7, 8 skinny legs.

That's not me, Millie thought.

Millie swished her tail
and guessed.

Mooooo!

Must be Spider!

Then, the artist painted someone
with two tall ears and
a fluffy white tail.

That's not me, thought Millie.

Millie swished her tail
and guessed.

Mooooo!

Must be Bunny!

The artist kept painting while Millie munched some grass, smelled the flowers, and played with her friends in the sunny meadow. When the artist was finished, he turned his painting for Millie to see.

Millie recognized her friends
Ladybug, Spider, and Bunny. And
right in the middle of the painting
was someone else—someone with
a white body and brown spots,
four legs, and a long tail.

Millie thought this someone looked
very happy—as happy as she was.

Millie swished her tail and guessed. . . .

For Graham

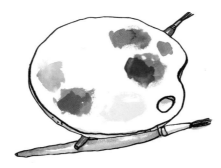

First edition 2003

Library of Congress Cataloging-in-Publication Data
Pedersen, Janet.
Millie in the meadow / Janet Pedersen. — 1st ed.
p.   cm.
Summary: As Millie the cow watches, an artist paints
pictures of some of the other meadow creatures —
and finally a picture of her as well.
ISBN 0-7636-1725-3
[1. Cows —Fiction. 2. Artists —Fiction. 3. Animals —Fiction.]
I. Title.
PZ7.P34233 Mi 2003
[E] — dc21   2001058114

2 4 6 8 10 9 7 5 3 1

Printed in Italy

This book was typeset in Gararond Medium.
The illustrations were done in gouache, watercolor,
crayon, and pen.

Candlewick Press
2067 Massachusetts Avenue
Cambridge, Massachusetts 02140

visit us at www.candlewick.com

jJFic